LIBRARY
RYERSON MIDDLE SCHOOL
222 Robinson Street
Hamilton   L8P 1Z9

CRABTREE CONTACT

THE HISTORY OF ROCK

Steven Rosen

Crabtree Publishing Company

www.crabtreebooks.com

Crabtree Publishing Company

www.crabtreebooks.com   1-800-387-7650
Copyright © **2009 CRABTREE PUBLISHING COMPANY**.

**Published
in Canada
Crabtree Publishing**
616 Welland Ave.
St. Catharines, ON
L2M 5V6

**Published in the
United States
Crabtree Publishing**
PMB16A
350 Fifth Ave., Suite 3308
New York, NY 10118

All rights reserved. No part of this publication may be reproduced, stored in a retrieval system or be transmitted in any form or by any means, electronic, mechanical, photocopying, recording, or otherwise, without the prior written permission of Crabtree Publishing Company.
Copyright © ticktock Entertainment Ltd 2009

Content development by Shakespeare Squared
www.ShakespeareSquared.com

Author: Steven Rosen
Project editor: Ruth Owen
Project designer: Simon Fenn
Photo research: Ruth Owen
Project coordinator: Robert Walker
Production coordinator: Katherine Berti
Prepress technicians: Samara Parent, Katherine Berti, Ken Wright

Thank you to
Lorraine Petersen
and the members
of nasen

Picture credits:
Getty Images: p. 5 (left), 10–11, 13; Michael Ochs Archives:
   p. 5 (right), 7, 9 (right), 12, 21; Popperfoto: p. 8, 14 (bottom);
   David Redfern: p. 20; Lorne Resnick: p. 24; Ebet Roberts:
   p. 25; Rolling Stones/GAB Archives: p. 15; Time & Life
   Pictures: p. 16
istockphoto: front cover
Redferns: Richard E Aaron: p. 23; Paul Bergen: p. 26 (bottom),
   28; Fin Costello: p. 31; Deltahaze Corporation: p. 6;
   GAB Archives: p. 17 (top); Elliott Landy: p. 18–19;
   Gered Mankowitz: p. 27; Chris Morphet: p. 14 (top)
Rex Features: R Bamber: p. 22
Shutterstock: p. 1, 2–3, 4–5, 6–7 (background), 9 (left),
   14 (background), 21 (background), 22–23 (background),
   26 (background)
WireImage: p. 29

Every effort has been made to trace copyright holders, and we apologize in advance for any omissions. We would be pleased to insert the appropriate acknowledgments in any subsequent edition of this publication.

Library and Archives Canada Cataloguing in Publication

Rosen, Steven, 1953-
      History of rock / Steven Rosen.

(Crabtree contact)
Includes index.
ISBN 978-0-7787-3823-7 (bound).--ISBN 978-0-7787-3844-2 (pbk.)

      1. Rock music--History and criticism--Juvenile literature.
2. Rock musicians--Juvenile literature. I. Title. II. Series: Crabtree contact

ML3534.R813 2009   j781.6609   C2008-907849-7

Library of Congress Cataloging-in-Publication Data

Rosen, Steven, 1953-
   History of rock / Steven Rosen.
         p. cm. -- (Crabtree contact)
   Includes index.
   ISBN 978-0-7787-3844-2 (pbk. : alk. paper) -- ISBN 978-0-7787-3823-7 (reinforced library binding : alk. paper)
   1. Rock music--History and criticism--Juvenile literature. 2. Rock musicians--Juvenile literature. I. Title. II. Series.

ML3534.R683 2009
781.6609--dc22

2008052409

CONTENTS

Chapter 1
What is Rock Music?..........4

Chapter 2
How it All Began...............6

Chapter 3
The 1960s.......................12

Chapter 4
The 1970s.......................20

Chapter 5
The 1980s.......................24

Chapter 6
The 1990s.......................26

Chapter 7
Rock Today.......................28

Need-to-know Words..........30

More Rock Styles/
Rock Music Online 31

Index......................32

CHAPTER 1

WHAT IS ROCK MUSIC?

Find a dictionary and look up the word "rock." It will say something like this:

A form of popular music with strong **vocals**, guitars, drums, and bass.

That's a correct but dull description. And rock music is anything but dull.

Rock music is powerful and exciting. When people listen to rock music, their hearts beat faster. Somehow, life seems better when you hear your favorite band.

Throughout rock's history, one group of musicians **influenced** the musicians that came after them.

But who are the most important musicians in rock's history?

Rock music fans will never stop arguing about this!

Chuck Berry

*Buddy Holly was the first musician to use two guitars, **bass**, and drums in his band.*

CHAPTER 2

HOW IT ALL BEGAN

Rock and roll came from mixing **country music** and the blues.

The blues belonged to African-American musicians. It came from songs sung by African-American farm workers.

Robert Johnson was a gifted **Delta blues** guitarist.

The Delta blues was a type of blues music played by musicians in the Mississippi Delta area.

Robert Johnson

Johnson only recorded 29 songs. He died in 1938 when he was just 27.

Johnson's music would influence future musicians such as the Rolling Stones, Cream, and later, Eric Clapton.

In the 1950s, parts of America suffered from segregation. African-American communities were separated from white communities. African-American people did not have the same rights as white people.

Gifted African-American musicians, such as Howlin' Wolf and Muddy Waters, could not get big **record labels** to listen to them.

So, small record labels formed such as King, Chess, and Aladdin. They recorded blues musicians and presented their music to the world.

Muddy Waters recording at Chess

In the 1950s, musicians began mixing the blues and country music to create something new—rock and roll.

On May 10, 1954, a band leader named Bill Haley recorded a song. It was called *(We're Gonna) Rock Around the Clock.*

Many people think this was the first rock and roll song.

Bill Haley and His Comets

In 1954, rock and roll's first superstar arrived on the scene. Elvis Presley was a poor boy from Tupelo, Mississippi.

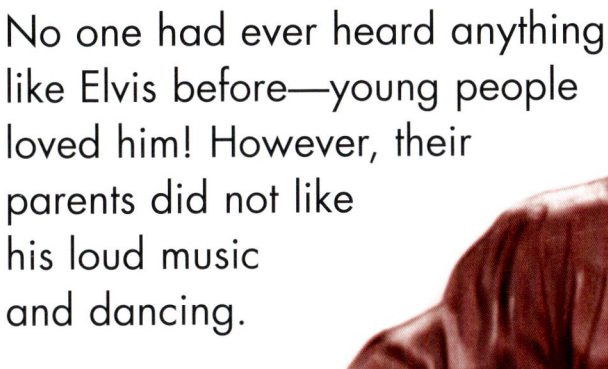

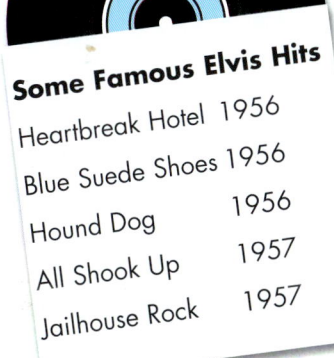

No one had ever heard anything like Elvis before—young people loved him! However, their parents did not like his loud music and dancing.

Some Famous Elvis Hits
Heartbreak Hotel 1956
Blue Suede Shoes 1956
Hound Dog 1956
All Shook Up 1957
Jailhouse Rock 1957

During his career, Elvis spent 80 weeks at the top of the music charts. He became known as "The King" to his fans.

Elvis "The King" Presley

From the beginning, rock and roll music was wild and loud.

The electric guitar became the main sound in this new style of music.

Ultimate Electric Guitars

Fender Stratocaster

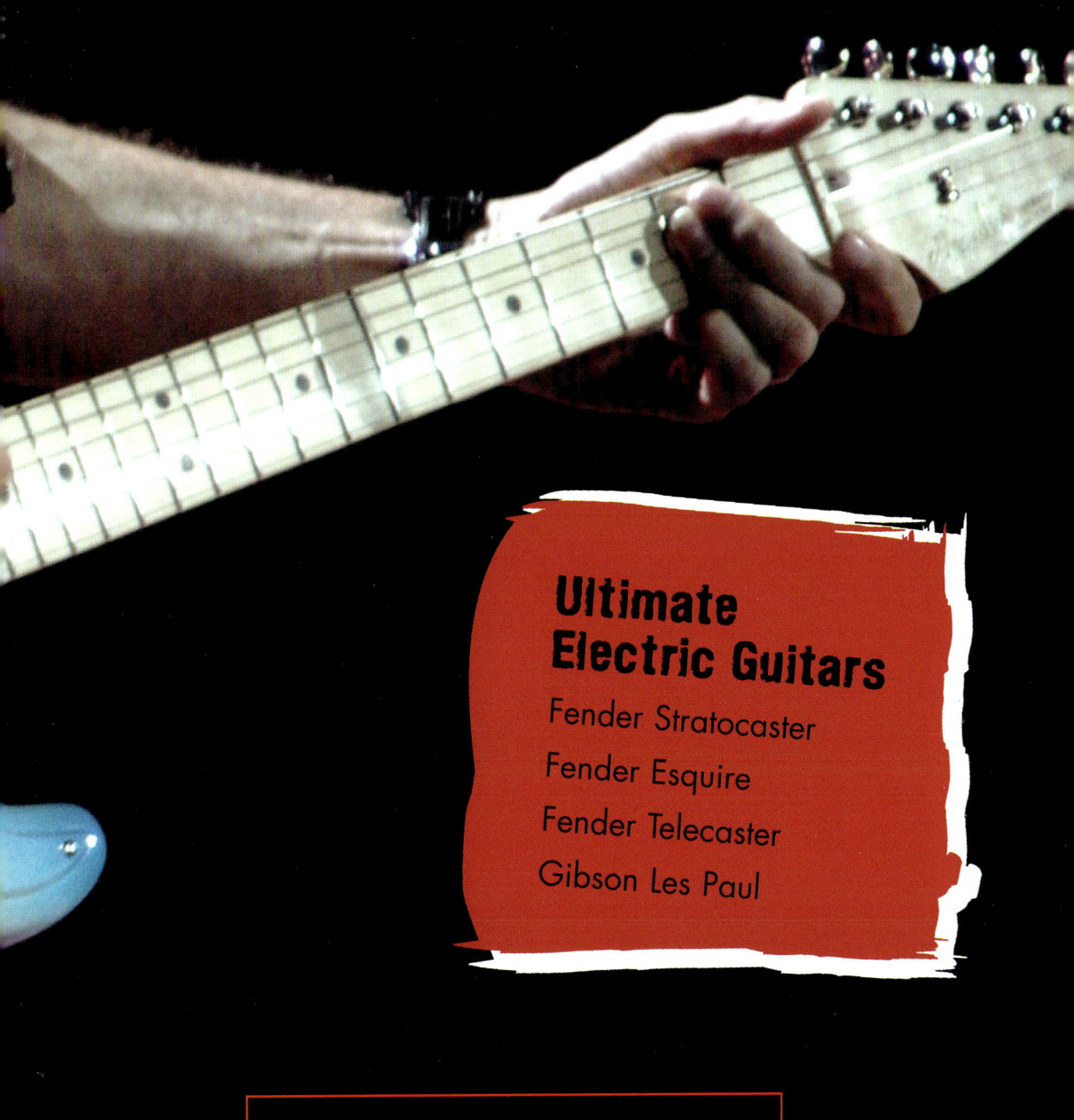

Fender Esquire

Fender Telecaster

Gibson Les Paul

Eric Clapton playing a later model Fender Stratocaster

Electric guitars were built by craftsmen in tiny workshops. Little did they know that these carved pieces of wood would become so important to rock and roll music.

CHAPTER 3
THE 1960s

Many people believe that the 1960s was the best time in rock and roll's history.

In California, the Beach Boys were singing about surfers, the beaches, hot rod cars, and young love.

The Beach Boys

English bands such as the Yardbirds, the Animals, and the Kinks were playing a type of English blues.

In Liverpool, England, four young musicians got together. They formed a band called The Beatles, which became one of the most famous bands in rock history.

Liverpool is a port city. In the 1960s, local sailors were bringing back records from America.

The Beatles were influenced by American artists, such as Chuck Berry and Elvis. The Beatles were one of the first groups to write their own songs. Their vocals and **vocal harmonies** made every song fresh and different.

John Lennon

Ringo Starr

Paul McCartney

George Harrison

The Who was an English band. They came out of a movement called "the Mods."

The Mods were English teenagers. They drove scooters and wore the latest fashions from London.

The Who's sound was built around the songs and guitar playing of leader Pete Townshend.

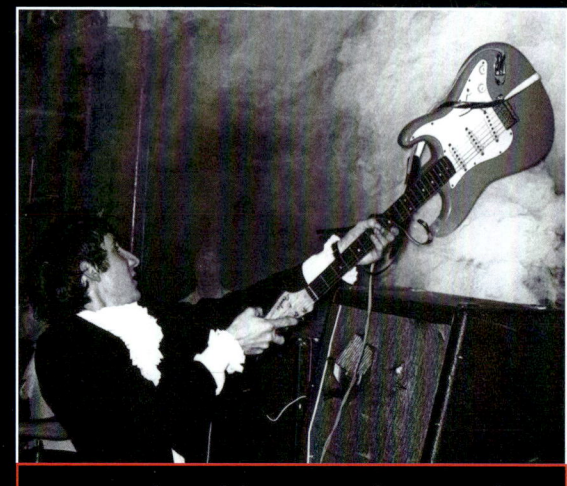

Townshend became famous for smashing up his guitars on stage.

1964—Mods in London

The Rolling Stones were another English band that listened to American blues.

Singer Mick Jagger and guitarist Keith Richards created a sound that was much bluesier than The Beatles.

Mick Jagger

Bill Wyman

Keith Richards

Charlie Watts

Brian Jones

The Rolling Stones

The Rolling Stones are still touring today!

The Beatles, The Who, and the Rolling Stones all toured America and became successful in the U.S. In America, this was called the "British Invasion."

By the late 1960s, American bands were trying out different styles of music.

Bands such as Love, Spirit, The Doors, and Buffalo Springfield were turning **folk rock** into psychedelic rock.

Psychedelic rock had a very dreamy feel to it. It mixed many music styles, from electronic music to music from India.

Jim Morrison, the lead singer of The Doors

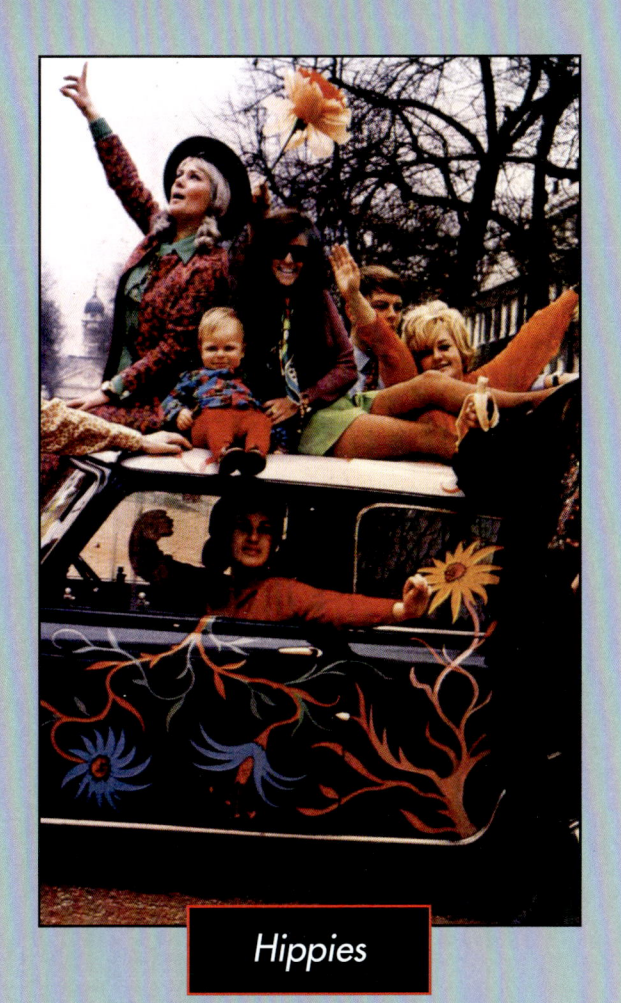

In 1967, the **Vietnam War** was raging.

Many young people were anti-war. They wanted a new way to live that promoted love and peace. Many young people became "hippies." They listened to psychedelic rock bands such as Quicksilver Messenger Service and Jefferson Airplane.

Hippies

In the late 1960s, guitar players were beginning to take the electric guitar to new limits. They used effects such as **fuzz** and **wah-wah pedals**. The "Guitar Hero" was born.

Guitar Heroes
- Jeff Beck (The Jeff Beck Group)
- Eric Clapton (Cream)
- Jimmy Page (Led Zeppelin)
- Ritchie Blackmore (Deep Purple)
- Peter Green (Fleetwood Mac)
- Mick Taylor (Rolling Stones)
- Robin Trower (Procol Harum)
- Paul Kossoff (Free).

Jimi Hendrix was a gifted American guitarist.

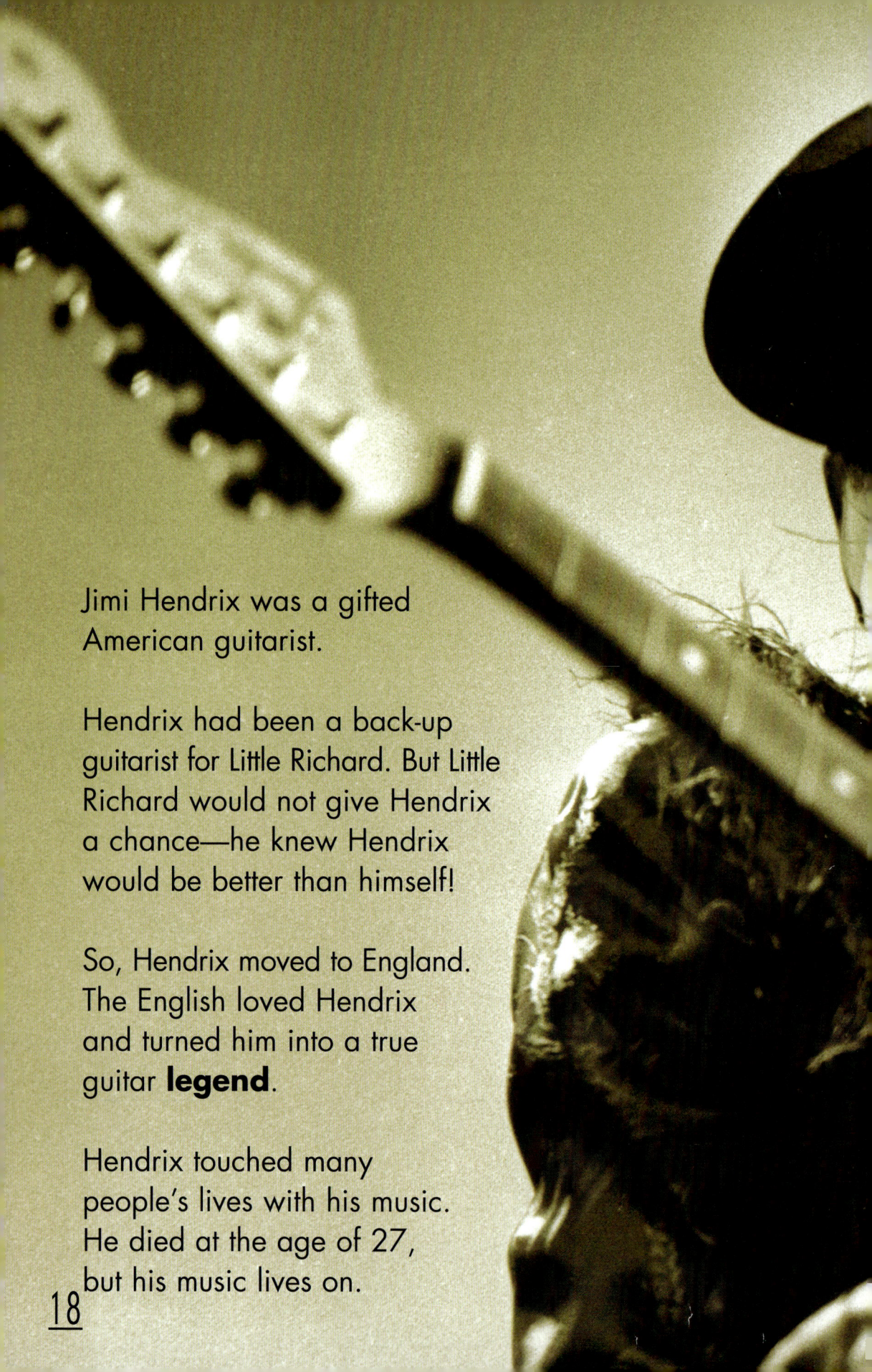

Hendrix had been a back-up guitarist for Little Richard. But Little Richard would not give Hendrix a chance—he knew Hendrix would be better than himself!

So, Hendrix moved to England. The English loved Hendrix and turned him into a true guitar **legend**.

Hendrix touched many people's lives with his music. He died at the age of 27, but his music lives on.

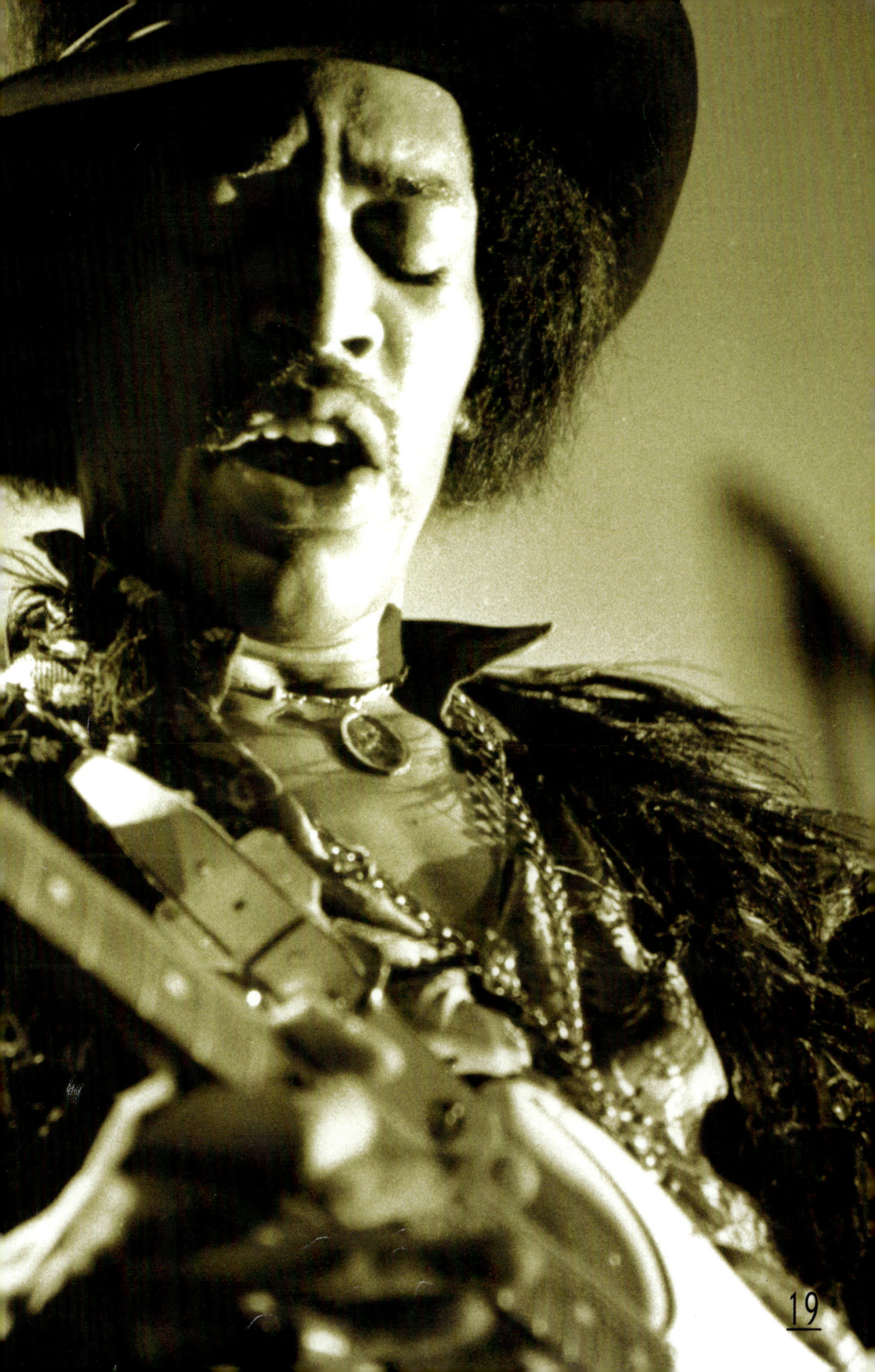

CHAPTER 4

THE 1970s

In the 1970s, **heavy metal** bands created huge walls of sound by turning **amplifiers** up to ten!

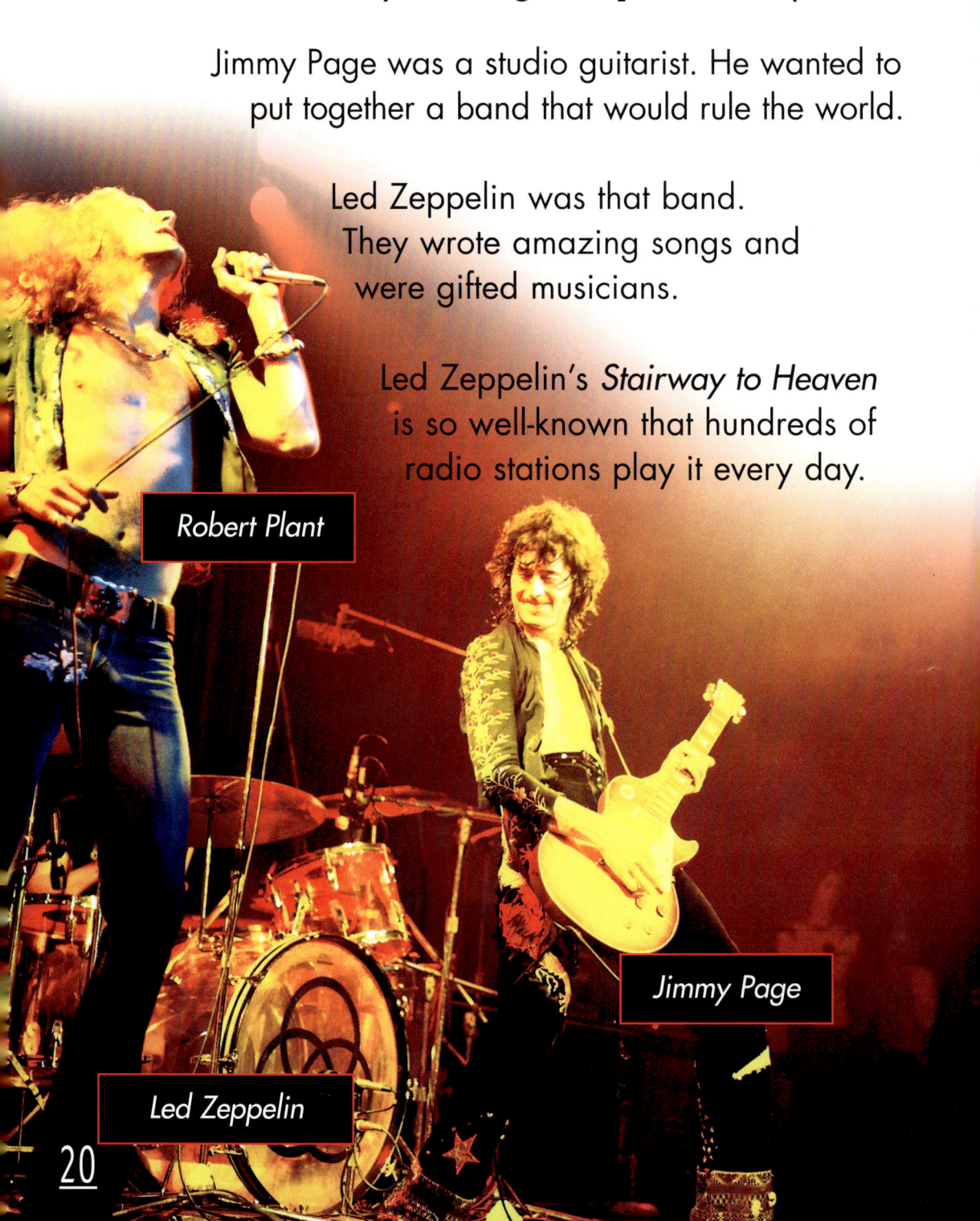

Jimmy Page was a studio guitarist. He wanted to put together a band that would rule the world.

Led Zeppelin was that band. They wrote amazing songs and were gifted musicians.

Led Zeppelin's *Stairway to Heaven* is so well-known that hundreds of radio stations play it every day.

Robert Plant

Jimmy Page

Led Zeppelin

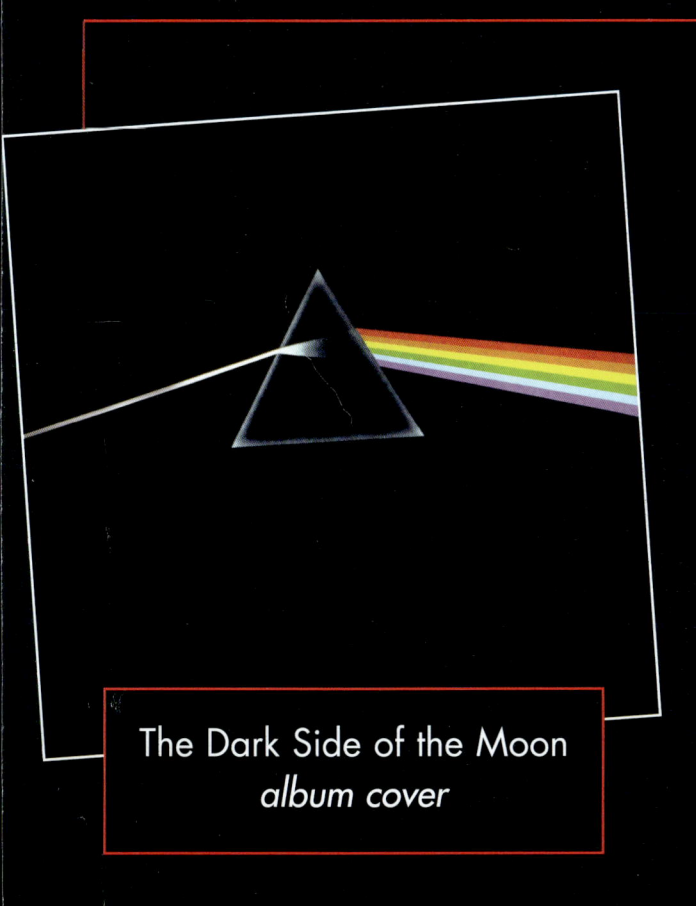

Heavy Metal Greats
- Black Sabbath
- Deep Purple
- Aerosmith
- Alice Cooper
- Van Halen
- Mountain
- Grand Funk Railroad

Progressive rock bands, such as Pink Floyd, were also emerging.

Progressive rock was more complex than normal rock. Bands used bits of classical music. They used keyboards to create the sounds of instruments such as violins and horns.

The Dark Side of the Moon *album cover*

In March 1973, Pink Floyd released *The Dark Side of the Moon*. The album stayed on the U.S. charts for 14 years!

The 1970s was also famous for "glam rock."

Bands such as the Sweet and T. Rex wore sequins, satin, make-up, and six-inch (15 cm) heels.

David Bowie puts on Ziggy Stardust make-up

David Bowie used pop and even theater in his music. When he performed he turned himself into different characters, such as Ziggy Stardust and the Thin White Duke. He used make-up and costumes to create these characters.

Then, in 1974, a new style of rock music was born in London—punk rock.

The guitars were out of tune. There were no melodies.

Sometimes the singer was singing one song while the band played another. Punk rock was anti-music!

England's Sex Pistols and The Clash were the most popular punk groups.

Johnny Rotten of the Sex Pistols

CHAPTER 5
THE 1980s

On August 1, 1981, MTV (Music Television) came on the air.

Musicians were now making videos of their performances. Now more than ever, a band's "look" was just as important as its sound.

Eddie Van Halen

Bands such as Bon Jovi, Mötley Crüe, and Van Halen looked great on TV. Their music became known as "hair metal" or "glam metal."

Guitarist Eddie Van Halen was a true guitar master. Other guitarists were amazed by his guitar skills.

In England, heavy metal groups such as Def Leppard, Iron Maiden, and Saxon became popular.

Their music was called the New Wave of British Heavy Metal (NWOBHM).

Iron Maiden

In the 1980s, the Irish band U2 had a major impact on rock music. Their music was built around the voice and songs of Bono, and the guitar sounds of The Edge.

CHAPTER 6: THE 1990s

In the cloudy, rainy city of Seattle, Washington, "grunge" was born.

Grunge was a little bit punk, a little bit heavy metal. Grunge musicians wore shabby clothes.

The music was moody-sounding. The songs were usually about being unhappy with yourself and the world around you.

Bands such as Alice in Chains, Soundgarden, Pearl Jam, and Nirvana played grunge music.

Nirvana in 1991

26

Oasis

In the UK, "Britpop" bands brought back the sounds of the Beatles, the Rolling Stones, and the Kinks.

The songs were catchy, and you could sing along to all the **lyrics**.

Britpop bands
- Oasis
- The Verve
- Radiohead
- Suede
- Pulp
- Blur

CHAPTER 7
ROCK TODAY

Today, the rock music of the past continues to influence new musicians.

Thrash metal bands, such as Mastodon and Slipknot, have been influenced by Led Zeppelin, Black Sabbath, and Iron Maiden.

Radiohead are a modern-day Pink Floyd.

Bands such as The Killers, Interpol, and the Editors are taking the punk rock of the 1970s and turning it into something new.

2008—the Editors play the Pinkpop Festival in Holland

Grunge has become post-grunge with bands such as the Foo Fighters, Collective Soul, and Seether.

Female artists such as KT Tunstall, Alanis Morissette, and Gwen Stefani have been influenced by many styles of music including punk.

KT Tunstall

Who will be the rock greats of the future?
Will your favorite band be remembered in ten years?

NEED-TO-KNOW WORDS

amplifier A piece of equipment that makes sounds louder. An electric guitar is plugged into an amplifier

bass A type of electric guitar with four strings and a lower sound than a normal electric guitar

country music A style of American music that began in the 1940s. It was originally played by poor, white musicians. It mixed little bits of the blues and folk music

Delta blues Blues music played by musicians living in the Mississippi Delta area

folk rock A simple style of music usually played by a single singer with a guitar. The songs are about the life of the singer and their community. Folk songs were a way to pass along history

fuzz A piece of equipment used with an electric guitar to make a fuzzy sound. The musician operates the equipment using a pedal

heavy metal A style of music with loud guitars and big amplifiers. The heavy metal singing style is almost like screaming

influence When one thing shapes or has an effect on something else

legend A story that is passed down through history and may be partly true and partly made up. Also, a person who has done something great and is remembered through history

lyrics The words of a song

record label A record company

Vietnam war A war in Asia between South Vietnam and North Vietnam. The war lasted from 1954 until 1975. America joined the war to help the South Vietnam army

vocal The singing part of a song

vocal harmony A singing part of a song that is different to the main vocal but blends with it to create a new sound

wah-wah pedal A piece of equipment used with an electric guitar to make a sound like crying. The musician operates the equipment using a pedal

MORE ROCK STYLES

- **New Wave**—In the late 1970s, bands such as Blondie, Talking Heads, and The Police turned punk rock into a music style that more people could enjoy and buy. This music was known as New Wave.

- **Goth rock**—The Cure played goth rock. They dressed up in black and looked like vampires.

- **Garage rock**—This style of music was played and recorded in garages in the 1960s. Today, it's back with bands such as The Hives and the White Stripes.

- **College rock**—This music grew up on college campuses across the U.S. and in the UK. College rock was a little bit punk and a little bit New Wave. It had a lot more melody, however. College rock bands include XTC, Edie Brickell and the New Bohemians, 10,000 Maniacs, and R.E.M.

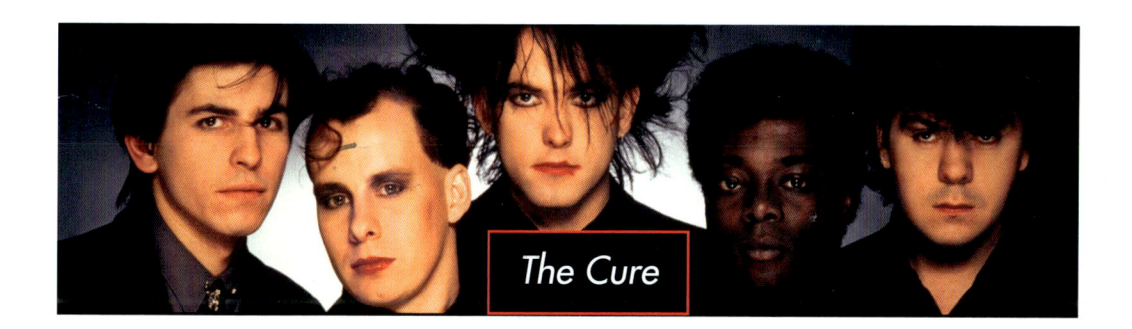

The Cure

ROCK MUSIC ONLINE

www.thebeatles.com/core/home/
A website all about The Beatles

www.trouserpress.com
Find out about alternative (different) styles of rock

Publisher's note to educators and parents:
Our editors have carefully reviewed these websites to ensure that they are suitable for children. Many websites change frequently, however, and we cannot guarantee that a site's future contents will continue to meet our high standards of quality and educational value. Be advised that children should be closely supervised whenever they access the Internet.

INDEX

10,000 Maniacs 31

A
Aerosmith 21
Animals, the 12

B
Beach Boys, the 12
Beatles, The 13, 15
Beck, Jeff 17
Berry, Chuck 5, 9, 13
Black Sabbath 21, 28
Blackmore, Ritchie 17
Blondie 31
blues 6–7, 8, 12, 15, 30
Blur 27
Bon Jovi 24
Bono 25
Bowie, David 22
Britpop 27
Buffalo Springfield 16
Byrds, the 15

C
Clapton, Eric 6, 10–11, 17
Clash, The 23
Cobain, Kurt 26
Collective Soul 29
college rock 31
Cooper, Alice 21
country music 8, 30
Cream 6, 17
Cure, The 31

D
Deep Purple 17, 21
Def Leppard 25
Doors, The 16

E
Edge, The 25
Edie Brickell and the New Bohemians 31
Editors, The 28

F
folk music 15, 16, 30
Foo Fighters 29

G
garage rock 31
glam (hair) metal 24
glam rock 22
Green, Peter 17
grunge 26, 29
guitar heroes 17, 18
Grand Funk Railroad 21

H
Haley, Bill 8
heavy metal 25, 30
Hendrix, Jimi 18–19
Hives, The 31
Holly, Buddy 5
Howlin' Wolf 7

I
Interpol 28
Iron Maiden 25, 28

J
Jefferson Airplane 17
Johnson, Robert 6

K
Killers, The 28
Kinks, The 12, 27
Kossoff, Paul 17

L
Led Zeppelin 17, 20, 28
Lennon, John 13, 26
Little Richard 9, 18
Love 16

M
Mastodon 28
Morrison, Jim 16
Mötley Crüe 24
Mountain 21

N
New Wave 31
Nirvana 26

O
Oasis 27

P
Page, Jimmy 17, 21
Pink Floyd 21, 28
Police, The 31
post-grunge 29
Presley, Elvis 9, 13
progressive rock 21
psychedelic rock 16–17
Pulp 27
punk rock 23, 28, 31

Q
Quicksilver Messenger Service 17

R
R.E.M. 31
Radiohead 27, 28
rock and roll 8–9
Rolling Stones, The 6, 15, 17
Rotten, Johnny 23

S
Saxon 25
Seether 29
Sex Pistols 23
Slipknot 28
Stefani, Gwen 29
Suede 27

T
Talking Heads 31
Taylor, Mick 17
thrash metal 28
Trower, Robin 17
Tunstall, KT 29

U
U2 25

V
Van Halen 21, 24
Van Halen, Eddie 24
Verve, The 27

W
Waters, Muddy 7
White Stripes, The 31
Who, The 14

X
XTC 31

Y
Yardbirds, The 12